OAKEE  DOAKEE

(Adventure One)

Titles available in the Oakee Doakee series
(in reading order):

Oakee Doakee and the Hate Wave

Oakee Doakee and the Ego Bomb

(available through *physical* and *cyber* bookstores everywhere!)

OAKEE DOAKEE

and the Hate Wave

Written and illustrated

by

Sir Ed Word

CheckPoint
Press

A Record of this Publication is available
from the British Library

ISBN 978-0-9551503-6-4

First Published 2008 by CheckPoint Press

CheckPoint Press
Dooagh
Achill Island
Westport
Co. Mayo
Republic of Ireland

Tel: 098 43779
Intl: +353 9843779
www.checkpointpress.com

This book is dedicated to
the little
Oakee Doakee
in you.

~CONTENTS~

This is the beginning of an amazing story about a little boy and his many adventures. His name is *Oakee Doakee* but his friends just call him Oakee. (When he's very naughty his teacher calls him Mr. Doakee.) Some people forget his name and call him Smokey or Pokey, but we'll remember it by writing it once in big letters like this:

****

The Adventures of

OAKEE DOAKEE

****

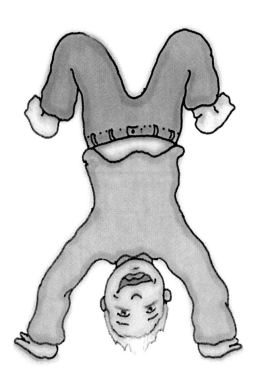

CHAPTER 1

The Heavens Beckon

One morning, Oakee woke up, washed his face, and sat down by the window to watch the sun peep over the horizon. As he sat there, his mind became silent and meditative and a lovely cool breeze filled the room. At the same time, he felt his heart fill up with joy. Then he started to hear beautiful music. He thought, *This must be the heavenly music of the angels.* It was so sweet, he prayed to the Heavenly Mother Empress, who he often dreamed of and felt in his heart, that he could go visit the angels to hear more of it. After breakfast, Oakee went outside to play because it was Sunday and there was no school. The sun was very warm this sunny Sunday, and the air smelled like sweet flowers and green grass.

As he was swinging on the swing, he looked up and noticed that there were no birds singing in the trees. As he sat there wondering where all the birds could be, a tiny rainbow colored hummingbird hummed by, just over his head.

"Wait!" he called. "Wait, little bird. Where are all the other birds today?"

The hummingbird stopped, flew in front of Oakee's nose and, hovering there, said in a tiny hummingbird voice, "Did you talk to me, little boy?"

"Yes I did. I thought maybe you know where all the birds have gone."

"All the birds? All the birds? All the birds have gone for their sun day singing lessons in the sun clouds," the hummingbird hummed.

"The birds have singing lessons?" asked Oakee surprised. "But who's their teacher?"

"We learn music from the gandharvas, of course," said the hummingbird a little impatiently.

Oakee happened to know that *gandharva* meant a special kind of angel that made music, because his father was a great scholar of history and mythology and other big amazing things, and Oakee had often eavesdropped on him and his colleagues as they discussed mysterious creatures and worlds. He also knew that gandharvas probably lived in the kingdom of the great king, Indra, beyond the sky.

"Now if you'll kindly excuse me, I'm late for the lesson,"

she added hastily, and as she buzzed away Oakee shouted after her:

"Oh, the gandharva angels? Please stop! Take me with you!"

"Sorry, that's not allowed," she called back. "But if you give me your name, I will see that King Indra is told of your request."

"I'm Oakee!" he shouted.

The hummingbird turned and disappeared into the big, blue sky. Oakee watched her go and, leaning back a little on his swing, wondered if King Indra would really let him visit his kingdom in the sun clouds.

CHAPTER 2

Passage to the Sky Worlds

Oakee was still swinging on the swing, when suddenly a powerful gust of wind almost blew him down. He turned around and saw a giant bird land in the garden. This was the most amazing person Oakee had ever seen! It looked like a bird, but it had a man's body with colorful, feathery short pants, and a shiny gold crown on its head. The birdman walked up to him, bowed his head with folded hands, and then smiled a big bird-like smile.

"Greetings little Oakee. I am Garuda, lord of all the birds. King Indra has asked me to bring you up for a visit to his kingdom in the sun clouds. Are you ready to come?"

Oakee just stared up at the royal visitor whose great, colorful wings shaded the whole garden from the light of the sun.

"Um," he tried hard to think of something to say, but he was completely thoughtless.

"Um," he said again. Then, with a jump of joy, he

shouted, "I'd love to come! I mean . . . I am ready, when you are."

Garuda knelt down on the grass and asked Oakee to climb up onto his big back. As soon as the little boy was holding on tight, Garuda moved his powerful wings, and with one great sweep they lifted up out of the garden, blowing up all the dry leaves and grass around them. In a moment they were high in the blue sky, and the swing, the garden, and the house looked like little toys far below. As they climbed higher and higher they passed through mountains of soft, white clouds. Sometimes they glided over deep cloud valleys, and Oakee thought he could see little villages here and there.

He was just wondering who could be living in these cloud villages, when they passed very close to a fluffy, white hillside where some cloud people were walking (or flying) along a narrow cloud road. The cloud people looked up and waved to Oakee. He smiled and waved back. There was a man and a lady and two children. They had white, shiny faces and two white wings on their backs. Their clothes were very colorful, and they wore delicate gold and silver jewelry. As they grew further away, they looked like four tiny rainbows, shimmering in the sunlight.

Garuda flew always up towards the sun. Oakee noticed that the wind on his face was getting warmer. The clouds were no longer deep and billowy, but more flat and layered. They passed through blanket after blanket of cloud, as if they were ascending the stairs of some magnificent house. Everything began taking on a golden hue and everything shone brightly in the sunshine. Oakee thought he could hear singing and music coming softly to them on the wind. He was very excited to see the singing angels. He listened carefully to catch more of that wonderful sound.

Garuda turned his big head and said in a loud, happy voice, "We are almost there!"

The air was now very warm as they brushed through the last layer of golden cloud. There, in the distance, shone a beautiful golden palace. The light of it was so bright that Oakee had to cover his eyes with his arm. The heavenly music was now clear and strong, and he was filled with excitement and wonder as he rushed towards King Indra's palace on the back of the mighty Garuda.

CHAPTER 3

Fun in the Sun Palace

In a few moments, they passed through the main gates of the palace and Garuda touched lightly down. Oakee jumped off his back and looked around. His eyes were accustomed to the light now, so he could see everything easily. They had landed in the middle of a great courtyard. At first nobody was there, but suddenly a guard wearing golden clothes and a golden helmet came out of a big doorway, and walked straight up to Oakee.

"Good morning, Oakee Doakee," said the handsome guard. "The king of the devas is expecting you. Please follow me."

Oakee looked up at the bird-god who had carried him all the way to this magical place.

Garuda smiled at him and said, "My master, Lord Vishnu, is waiting for me up in Vaikunta, the higher heaven. I will meet you again some other time."

Oakee gave him a big hug and watched as his giant

friend flew away into the sky. Then he turned and followed the guard through the doors.

They walked along a huge hallway. It was lined with unusual statues and vases and other ornaments. Sunlight poured in through windows near the ceiling. Oakee found it all very beautiful, but best of all was the beautiful singing that echoed everywhere and seemed to be coming from all around him. The music became louder and louder until they finally reached the end of the passage where two guards stood before a great doorway.

Oakee's mouth opened wide with awe and amazement as the doors swung open. He stood at the entrance of a royal reception room, so big that he couldn't see the far side. Music, sunshine, and countless wonderful people and creatures filled the whole place. There were strong, dignified devas (gods of the elements) who looked like stars or suns in their shiny jewelry. There were laughing, dancing animals, some of which, like the unicorns, Oakee had only read about in fairy tales. There were thousands of varieties of birds, all singing in perfect harmony; and colorful angels with gold or silver wings; and white angels with pure white or pinkish wings. Some of the angels played harps, flutes or bells. Others that sat on the floor playing drums and harmoniums looked a bit like naughty monkeys. *The birds are really learning to sing!* thought Oakee.

The next moment, he was surprised to find himself in a long chain of dancers pushing its way through the crowds. The line of happy souls became two huge circles, one going around the other in the opposite direction. It became a stick-dance with everyone clicking their sticks against those of their next partner.

Oakee was having so much fun dancing with a friendly lion and some baby angels, that he didn't notice when the music stopped and everyone began sitting down. All of a sudden, he found himself sitting on the big, soft lap of the lion, and silence filled the hall. Then the most beautiful sound of all came as all the hosts of heaven sang the glorious Sahasrara mantra-hymn of the thousand rainbow petals, in honor of their Heavenly Mother Empress. Oakee was filled with such an overwhelming feeling of sweet peace, that he closed his eyes and fell asleep, there among his new friends in the Great Hall of King Indra's palace beyond the sky.

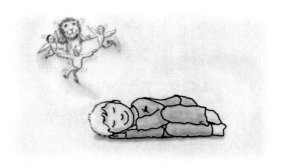

CHAPTER 4

The Rulers of the Lower Heavens

When he awoke, Oakee found himself on a soft, white bed in a big, quiet room. All the walls had high windows, and through all the windows shone warm sunlight. He had just sat up, when a colorful little bird flew in from the next room. It was the hummingbird he had met in his garden!

"It's nice to see you again, Oakee. I saw you at the music session. You were dancing up a storm. If you're well rested, the king would like to see you now. Please follow me." And, without giving him a chance to answer, the speedy little bird rushed out the way she had come.

Oakee followed her as fast as he could. They passed through two rooms similar to the one he had woken up in, and then down a wide hallway, which led to a golden door. The door was open, and as he approached it, Oakee saw that he was coming back to the Great Hall – not where he had entered for the music celebration, but through a side door near the other end. The hall was now empty, except for a beautifully decorated dais near the end wall. On the dais were two thrones, and on the thrones sat the two loveliest people Oakee had ever seen. Their faces shone with an ancient, heavenly light. As he came closer, one of them stood up and smiled at him. It was King Indra, himself!

"Welcome to Amaravati, dear Oakee. We are honored by your presence."

Oakee walked slowly forward, a little bit embarrassed, because he thought the king was thanking him for bringing 'presents', which he hadn't.

"Um, I forgot to bring some presents . . ." he started to say, when the king happily interrupted him:

"This is the first visit we have ever had by such a dharmatma as yourself, and the Paramchaitanya – the cool, life-giving vibrations that flow from your heart – brings us more joy than any earthly gifts."

"What's a 'dharmatma'?" asked Oakee humbly.

Now the other person, who was still sitting down, held her arms out to Oakee. He was a bit stunned by her great beauty and her shining personality, but he summoned up enough courage to walk right up to her. Much to his surprise, she picked him up onto her lap and smiled a heavenly smile in his face. Then she spoke to him in a voice like honey:

"Little prince and son of our Heavenly Mother, I am Indrani, Queen of Devalok. What my husband is trying to tell you, is that we have been greatly blessed by our Heavenly Mother Empress, that one of Her special children – one of Her innocent Earth children – has asked to come and visit us. Never before have we enjoyed such a privilege. We hope that you enjoyed the music of our gandharvas, and we apologize for any discomfort you may have had as our guest."

Oakee tried to say that he had been very comfortable, but the queen just smiled and continued.

"Your coming to us is very auspicious, especially at this important time."

Oakee was going to ask what 'auspicious' meant, but he didn't want to interrupt again.

"Oakee Doakee, we need you to do a very special job. No one else here is capable of carrying out such a task as this, so we are relying on you to help us. Would you like to try?"

"Does it mean going on a big adventure?" asked Oakee eagerly.

"Yes. A very big adventure," answered the beautiful queen.

"Okay! I'll do it!" exclaimed Oakee. And, with that, Queen Indrani and her Lord thanked him with a big hug, and told of the great adventure that awaited him.

CHAPTER 5

Preparations for the Journey

"Before we send you on your mission, we have a special treat for you," said the queen. She nodded her head to an attendant who had just entered the hall with a silver tray. On the tray was a silver cup, which the queen took and offered to Oakee. As Oakee put the cup to his mouth he smelt a heavenly perfume; and as he drank the creamy liquid inside it, he felt like he was swimming in a pool of happiness. When he finished, he handed the cup to the attendant, and smiled at his hosts.

"This is Amrit, the food of the gods," explained Indrani. "We hope it will give you enough strength for the task ahead." She signaled to another attendant who brought a chair that looked like a small throne, for Oakee to sit on.

"Dearest Oakee," began King Indra, "since long ago, we devas have often been at war with the wicked demons, the rakshasas, who sought every opportunity to terrorize the good people and fight with us. Now, by the grace of our

Heavenly Mother and Her power of Love, almost all the rakshasas are gone. . . ."

"You don't have to fight the rakshasas anymore?" interrupted Oakee, who knew the legends about these monsters.

"No. No more fighting. The rakshasas are gone because the Love of our Heavenly Mother has made the good people strong, and the bad ones weak. But a serious problem is still troubling us here in Devalok. Human beings still have too much ego – that hot, selfish bully in the head that does not mind hurting others; so much ego that the heat is beginning to burn our kingdom. Our flowers and trees are dying and my favorite rain clouds, Avartaka and Pushkala, are almost dried out. Even on the Earth, all the ice is melting and the deserts are expanding. This Hate Wave is crushing the love in the hearts of everyone. Only an enlightened soul, an innocent Earth child, who is free from the chains of ego, can help us all. This is why your coming has filled us with so much hope."

"Well, I'm just a little boy, but my morning meditation makes me strong as the wind. Hanuman told me – he's my monkey dream-friend and commander of the angel armies – and he should know 'cause he's the son of the Wind," proclaimed Oakee.

"Yes, I have no doubt that you are even as strong as your good friend Lord Hanuman, himself," said King Indra merrily. "He is called by us as the lion-hearted Lord of the Angels, Archangel Gabriel, Hermes or Mercury, and anyone who wins his heart becomes invincible."

The queen noticed that Oakee didn't understand the word 'invincible', so she explained to him that it means *nobody can hurt you.*

The King stood up slowly and took Oakee's hand. "Follow me out to the garden," he said.

Suddenly, the wall behind the dais began to shimmer and fade, and a few seconds later Oakee was led down some elegant steps into a heavenly garden. The colors and shapes and smells filled him with wonder and made him almost forget to breathe.

"Wow! This is even nicer than our garden!" exclaimed Oakee. "Do you have swings, too?"

"We have no swings in the Nandana Garden," said the King, "but here is something much better." And, as they walked around the end of a flowery wall, Oakee saw a sight that made him forget everything else he had seen. It was a giant white elephant with four huge tusks and beautiful, shining ornaments.

"Oakee Doakee, meet Airavata, my vahana-vehicle. He will be *your* vehicle and servant for the great journey that lays before you."

And as King Indra spoke these words, Oakee felt something like butterflies in his stomach; but he quietly thanked his Heavenly Mother Empress in his heart, and wondered what amazing things would happen next.

CHAPTER 6

The Wish-Fulfilling Cow

"Do not feel shy," said Indrani. "You can go closer." So, Oakee walked right up to Airavata, who gently touched Oakee's nose with his long trunk. Oakee looked into the elephant's big eye and thought he was smiling.

"I think he likes me," he said. "But how will I get up on him?"

Before he could get an answer, the big trunk reached under him and lifted him up, up, up to the king's throne on Airavata's back.

"Wow!" exclaimed Oakee. "This is great!"

From this high position he could see far and wide over the heavenly garden. For the first time since he arrived at Amaravati, he noticed the harsh heat in the air. And now, as he looked carefully around, he saw that the flowers and trees actually looked tired and weak.

"We wish you good fortune and success!" called out the King.

"But I don't even know where to go or what to do!" called Oakee back, a little bit anxiously.

"No fear, little prince," said the Queen of Amaravati. "Airavata knows the way. All arrangements have been made. You will travel on Indradhanush, the Great Rainbow."

"The way to where?" asked Oakee. But the only answers he got were smiles and waves from King Indra and his shakti, his powerful consort, who looked smaller and smaller as Oakee and his royal vahana rose up into the sky.

As he looked down, Oakee thought he could see a little spot of color coming up to them. In a few seconds he realized it was not a spot, but his hummingbird friend, who flew quickly up to Oakee's nose.

Hovering there, she hummed, "Hi Oakee! Remember me? We met in your garden and in King Indra's palace. My name's Lulu but you can call me Lu. I've been sent to help you on your great mission. Isn't it all so exciting?"

Oakee tried to answer, but couldn't fit a word in because she was talking so fast.

"Look! Over there," Lulu continued, "there's the great Indradhanush. We're almost on it!"

Oakee looked up and saw the top of the fattest, most

colorful rainbow he had ever seen. They were flying quickly through light, golden clouds. Now Lulu was sitting on Oakee's knee as they soared through the sky on top of the white elephant. Suddenly they passed through the crest of a big cloud, and in the next moment they found that they were coming to rest on a massive highway of color. It was so wide that Oakee didn't at first notice that it was not flat, but round, like the body of a huge, colorful snake.

"Oh look!" exclaimed Lulu. "It has all the same colors as me." And she flew up to proudly show off her bright, little feathers.

But Oakee wasn't watching her, because something else had caught his attention.

"It looks like we have a visitor," he said in a whisper.

Oakee, Lulu, and Airavata all watched quietly as the stranger approached them. It was a white cow, and it walked very slowly across the rainbow road towards them. When it came very close and stopped, Lulu spoke out to it:

"Hello friend! We are children of the Heavenly Mother Empress on an important mission for King Indra, Lord of the Devas. Please tell us who you are and what you want."

The cow lifted its big, brown eyes to the bird and the child on the elephant's back, and said in a lovely, deep voice:

"I am called Kamadhenu, the wish-fulfilling cow. I have come to offer a wish to Prince Oakee Doakee. He may ask for anything, and it will come true."

CHAPTER 7

The Great Rainbow Ride

Through Oakee's mind, there flashed all the wonderful things he had ever enjoyed, or hoped to someday enjoy. He thought of mountains of ice cream and rivers of cola. He wondered what it would be like to wake up every morning in Disneyland and play with his favorite cartoon heroes all day; or how it would be to drive trains and ships around the world and be called *Captain* by everyone. More and more ideas crowded his imagination, until a little humming sound in his ear awoke him from his daydream. It was Lulu urging him to give an answer to the wish-fulfilling cow. Oakee's face turned suddenly pink as he remembered Kamadhenu, who stood looking patiently up at him. Just then, the importance of his mission and all the words of King Indra and his consort came back to him.

He looked over at the little hummingbird and again at the cow, and slowly said:

"Please, beautiful cow, I do have a wish: I wish that

all the heat and hate of people's egos will be cooled off by the cool breeze of our Heavenly Mother's love, and that our mission will help this to come true. This I wish with all my heart."

As he finished speaking, a cool, divine wind of Vibrations poured out from his hands and the top of his head and blew in circles all around him, the bird, the elephant, and the cow.

Then Kamadhenu smiled a big smile and said:

"You have wished well, little prince. Good-bye and good fortune!" And with that, the white Cow of Heaven slowly changed into a white cloud and rose into the sky.

Oakee watched until the cloud had drifted out of sight, and was about to ask Lulu what to do next, when something appeared in his hand. He was so surprised that he almost dropped it. Oakee couldn't believe his eyes . . . it was an ice cream cone! He enjoyed it very much and so did his friends! Airavata carefully took a bit on the end of his trunk and brought it down into his mouth, but Lulu got the ice cream all over her little face as she tried to eat it with her delicate beak! After they finished their treat, and Oakee had cleaned the little bird's face, the great white elephant began walking forward. In a moment, they were sliding down the smooth rainbow, and getting faster and faster.

"Hold on!" peeped Lulu, "We're go-i-i-ing!"

"Going where?!" shouted Oakee.

"Did I forget to tell you?" Lulu called back from under his arm, "to Bhogavati, the city of the Water King, under the ocean! We-e-e-e-e!"

They rushed on and on down the giant rainbow, and saw many wonderful sights on the way. Between mountains of white cloud, the sunshine sometimes sparkled on invisible ice-crystals in the air, which danced about the travelers like millions of tiny fairies. Once, Oakee noticed a flock of great birds passing far below them.

"Those are albatrosses," Lulu called out, "They are good friends of the Water King."

Evening was approaching and the clouds exchanged their whiteness for beautiful hues of pink, orange and yellow, with dark walls of shadow rising up behind them. Suddenly, flashes of lightning appeared like a fantastic fireworks display.

"Wow!" exclaimed Oakee.

"King Indra is showing us some of his powers," called Lulu, "and ridding our path of all troubling evils!"

Soon they could see the endless, dark ocean below

them as they rushed full speed towards it on their giant slide, the Indradhanush Rainbow.

CHAPTER 8

Through the 'Pot of Gold'

As they came closer to the surface of the ocean, they saw the last edge of the sun about to slip down under the soft blankets of the horizon. Just then, another unexpected thing happened. Until now they had been riding on *top* of the wide tube of the rainbow; but now they seemed to be sinking *into the middle* of it. Soon they found themselves, still speeding down towards the ocean, completely protected in the middle of the rainbow. It was almost dark outside as the waves of the great sea appeared closer and closer, and the brightness of the colors around them was gone. Oakee and Lulu braced themselves for a big splash as they saw the water just before them. They closed their eyes and held their breath as they reached the foamy sea – but nothing happened. They were still sliding down inside the rainbow, completely dry under the water!

A whole new world opened up around them. At first, all they could see were little sparks of phosphorous in the dark, swirling water, and one or two shining eels swimming about. But much to their surprise, the deeper they went, the more they could see. In a little while it was light enough to see schools of colorful fish and beds of seaweed floating around. Their rainbow was getting all its color back in the soft light that seemed to be coming up from the bottom of the sea. Before long, they noticed that they were heading towards a glowing bubble that looked very tiny, far, far below them. This *bubble* was in fact a great dome over the city called Bhogavati where King Varuna, the guardian of all the waters, lived with his people.

Oakee was the first one to speak after their long ride.

"Look Lulu. The light is coming from that place down there, just where the rainbow ends."

"I hope it's not too wet," replied Lulu, "I've never tried flying underwater."

They could see everything clearly now: the crystal blue-green water, countless fish and other interesting sea creatures, and beautiful water trees and flowers. Airavata had somehow slowed down as they neared their destination. In a moment they were passing through the roof of the city and down into a lovely garden. In the center of the garden was a huge golden vessel where the rainbow came to an end. As they gently touched down inside this big pot, two curved, golden doors opened up on one side of it.

"Hey! This must be the famous 'pot' at the end of the rainbow," exclaimed Oakee. "But really it's a *golden pot*, not a *pot of gold*!"

Lulu was happy to be able to fly again.

"It's not wet here at all," she hummed merrily.

Airavata walked slowly out through the doors into the garden where so many wonderful things met Oakee's eyes that he didn't know where to look first.

There was a great crowd of unusual people assembled there to meet him; some were standing on dry ground, and others were watching him from great pools of seawater (which were actually connected to the ocean, outside). Some of the people were half fish; others were riding on big seahorses; and many looked like the celestial devas he had seen in the court of King Indra, only a little less celestial and a little more underwaterish.

Then, the biggest and most royal looking of the devas stepped forward, and said with a loud, jolly voice:

"Beloved Oakee Doakee, I am King Varuna! I and my people welcome you with open hearts to Bhogavati!"

Then he gave such a big laugh that everyone joined in,

including Oakee, who laughed until his belly hurt!

CHAPTER 9

Under-Sea Surprises

When everyone had stopped laughing, King Varuna spoke again, "Dear guests, please follow us to the sea-fruit tree orchard where our picnic is being prepared."

Oakee's tummy rumbled when he heard the word 'picnic'. The ice cream cone they had eaten on top of the rainbow had been tasty, but, shared three ways, it was not very filling. As they all moved across the garden, he began to wonder what kind of food would be served down here. *Maybe everything tastes fishy and salty*, he thought, as he looked around at all the mermen and mermaids and other sea-people. But he didn't have to wonder long. Soon he was being helped down from the elephant's back onto a wide, green lawn of soft, rubbery grass. Overhead hung the branches of strange trees full of colorful fruit. Oakee sat on the grass next to the king, with Lulu on his lap. First they ate some of the fruit, which was not salty at all, but sweet and juicy. Then they had something like noodles with cheese, and some kind of vegetable. Normally, Oakee didn't like vegetables, but these ones had such a rich, pleasant flavor that he even asked for more. There was something cool to drink afterwards, and then best of all: ice cream for dessert.

The meal had been accompanied by the melodic sound of conversation, most of which Oakee couldn't understand; but now the atmosphere grew quieter and quieter, and he noticed that everyone was lying down when they'd finished. Oakee also lay down and fell fast asleep.

When he awoke, the first thing Oakee saw from where he lay on the grass was the back of the king who still sat next to him, and the edge of his big beard which moved as he talked. When Oakee sat up, he saw that it was Lulu to whom he spoke. Lulu sat on the hand of the Sea King, listening as he explained something to her.

When he noticed that Oakee had woken up, he smiled and said, "I hope you have eaten and slept well, Prince Oakee. You have another long journey ahead of you, as I have just been explaining to your little companion."

"Um, yes, sir. I'm sure, sir," nodded Oakee a little sleepily. And then, after a thoughtful moment, he added, "Why does everyone call me 'prince'?"

"As a son of the Heavenly Mother, who is Divine Empress of all the universes, you are indeed worthy of this title. Do not the boys and girls of your world call yourselves so?"

"Well, no. Most of them don't know about our Heavenly Mother Empress. But I'm sure if they met Her in their hearts they would also realize they are Her princes and princesses."

"Many will. Of that, you may be certain," replied King Varuna sincerely. "All our efforts strive to that same end."

Just then, a messenger came running up to them. Quite out of breath, he quickly reported something to the king in a language that Oakee didn't understand. King Varuna's face grew dark and solemn as the messenger spoke. Then, after a short silence, the Lord of the Waters turned to Oakee and said:

"There is no time to lose. The Mother Earth, Her heavens, and Her water kingdoms are in great peril and suffering grievously. The hate wave from the collective ego is increasing at an alarming rate, and threatens to suffocate all sweetness and beauty in the three worlds. You must set out at once. Everything depends upon the success of your mission!"

CHAPTER 10

Final Instructions

"There is a lake," continued the Sea King, "at the foot of the holy mountain Kailash, up in the earthly home of the Heavenly Mother. This blessed lake was created at the beginning of time by the goddess Alaknanda. She is the pure desire of Lord Shiva, who is the protector of pure Heart-Spirit. She is known as Ganga on the Earth. She came to lead the seekers of Truth back home to the realm of their Heavenly Mother in their hearts, by bringing the cooling Divine Vibrations from heaven down to the Earth. Alaknanda means that she came down like water from the Sahasrara, the top of the head, of her Lord in the high heavens. The first place that she touched on the Earth was at the foot of Lord Shiva's throne, Mount Kailash, in the Himalayan Mountains. This mountain range is the high and holy Sahasrara Lotus of the Earth. There she formed the magical lake Manasarovar. That is your final destination. Airavata knows the way to the top of your world. Do you have any questions?"

Oakee looked over at Lulu, then down at the grass, then back at the King's serious face, and said, "I can't think of anything right now, sir."

"Then let us take the mantra-hymn to Lord Ganesha, the elephant-headed protector of the Earth, and the remover of obstacles."

They sang the sacred hymn, and as they did so, a divine breeze filled the garden where they sat. Any worries that had begun to tug at Oakee's heart, now vanished. He stood up and bowed to the King, who smiled again and kissed the top of the little boy's head. Airavata, who looked like a snowy mountain decorated with golden sunshine, walked to Oakee and lifted him up to his back with his trunk. Lulu flew up and sat on Oakee's lap. As they all moved across the garden, with King Varuna's hand on the side of Oakee's royal vehicle leading the crowd, Oakee began for the first time to feel like a real prince.

Before the three travelers entered the great golden pot, the King looked up at Oakee and said, "Fear not, little one. You are destined to succeed with your mission. But if you should ever find yourself in danger, simply take the name of Lord Hanuman. He and his angel army will come to your aid!"

Airavata turned around in the pot to face the Lord of the Waters and his people. As the doors slowly closed, Oakee watched all the loving faces and waved farewell to them. In a moment, he and his companions were flying again, but this time they were going up the rainbow. The bubble of Bhogavati became smaller and smaller below them, and the light of it became less and less. Again the rainbow was invisible as they traveled up through the darkness.

After some moments of silence, Lulu started to sing:
"Far, far away
At the top of the world
Where the holy ones pray
And the four winds do swirl,
The Father of all
Meditates in the OM,
While the Mother does call
All the lambs to come home."

"That's a beautiful song, Lulu. Where did you learn it?" asked Oakee.

"My mommy used to sing it to me when I was a baby bird," Lulu replied. "I just remembered it now. But that's just the beginning. I forget the rest."

Soon they were surprised by a warm, salty wind on their faces, and the sound of rolling waves on a beach.

"We've left the rainbow!" exclaimed Oakee. "I think Airavata is wading through the water up to dry ground."

At first it was still too dark to see anything, but then they noticed a soft yellow light coming from the eastern horizon. The sun was waking up.

"Look!" cried Lulu. "Lord Surya the sun god is bringing the morning!"

CHAPTER 11

The Jingle Jungle

As they approached the dry ground, they saw a dark line of trees rising before them.

"Look! This must be the Jingle Jungle!" exclaimed Lulu, who was by now getting very exited about the whole adventure.

"The Jingle Jungle?" remarked Oakee inquisitively. "Why's it called like that?"

"A long, long time ago, the celestial friends of the holy men hung little bells in all the trees here to warn these saints of the presence of evil rakshasas who came to disturb their godly rituals," explained Lulu.

"Oh, dear. Do you suppose there might still be some of those yucky creatures around?" asked Oakee.

"Don't worry," said Lulu. "You know what King Indra said. The rakshasas are gone. The only yucky creatures we're likely to find here now are mosquitoes!"

When they reached the beach, Airavata set Oakee

gently down and went in search of breakfast. He soon returned with a trunk full of dry fruit, which he shared with his little friends who lay on the warm sand. They wanted to stay and watch the sunrise, but Airavata was soon urging Oakee to return to his place on the elephant's great back. With his passengers securely in their places, he advanced steadily in the direction of the jungle that he had visited many times in the past with his master, the Lord of the Devas.

"I've heard lots and lots about this place," boasted Lulu. "It's here you can find the most beautiful trees in the world: Bakula, Ashvattha, Ashoka, Palasa, Kadamba, Panasa, Kritamala, Madhuka, and Karavira; and they all blossom and their perfumes rise right up into the heavens. There are supposed to be fountains of cool water that gush up from underground springs . . ."

As Lulu continued with her important lesson, Oakee's attention was drawn away to their new surroundings. They had just entered the jungle and somehow its appearance didn't match Lulu's enthusiastic description.

After some time, Oakee interrupted his little friend, "Hey, Lu. I think there's something very wrong here."

The little bird stopped talking and looked around. The

beautiful dream world that she had been describing turned out to be more like a nightmare. The further they went from the ocean, the drier, blacker, and uglier the jungle became. Dead plants lying across their path crunched beneath Airavata's feet, and a blanket of heat was slowly pressing down from above the treetops.

"The curse of ego has even reached here," said Oakee, sadly.

"I should have guessed," said Lulu. "The panasa fruit we ate on the beach should have been round and juicy, not dry and wrinkled. What if we get to the magic lake too late? What if the lake is all dried up?"

"Why doesn't Airavata just fly there?" asked Oakee.

"King Varuna told me that the heat of the sky is growing so quickly that we will have to travel by land – and under the trees wherever possible," answered Lulu.

They traveled a long time in silence. The heat was all around them now, and they were always thirsty. They drank from bags of juice given to them by the sea-people, but it would not last them very long. As they went, they noticed no signs of life, not even a mosquito, and no jingle bells could be seen or heard.

It was twilight, and Oakee and Lulu were half asleep

when a sudden sound shocked them into wakefulness. Someone was shouting. They looked ahead and saw a small figure flying towards them. It was a vanadevata, a tree-dryad, who guarded the forest.

"Go back!" it shouted. "Run for your lives! It's coming!"

CHAPTER 12

Dancing With the Monkey-Angels

Oakee and Lulu just stared at the little creature with their mouths open. They were upset enough by its startling approach, but the fact that something terrible was following it made them too frightened to speak.

Finally, Oakee asked, "Wh-what's coming?"

The trembling little face in front of him said, "Oh-h-h the FIRE! The FIRE! Get away if you can!"

At that moment, Airavata gave a great trumpeting noise with his trunk straight up in the air, as the dusky darkness around them was replaced by a wild light. There ahead, through the branches and trunks of the trees, they could see tongues of flames tearing their way through the dry forest. The dryad screamed and flew away to the sea. Airavata stomped his foot on the earth and trumpeted again. The noise of the fire grew louder. Everything was happening too fast for Oakee.

"What should we do? What should we do?" he

shouted.

"Call the angels!" shouted Lulu back.

So, Oakee took a deep breath, and as loud as he could, called out: "HANUMANA-A-A-A!!!"

Suddenly, a cool wind came blowing from the sea, far, far away, and hit the wall of fire like a tidal wave. In the same moment, thousands of white monkeys dropped down out of the trees and rushed towards the burning woods. Leading them was a big monkey wearing a golden crown. They could hear him shout something as he charged the fire.

He called: "**JAI SHRI MATAJI!**" (meaning GLORY and VICTORY to the GREAT MOTHER) and in such a deep, powerful voice, that Oakee felt strength and even joy coming back into his heart.

In fact, Oakee now felt so strong and happy, that he jumped right down from the giant elephant's back, and ran after the monkey-angels, calling out, "I'm coming Hanuman!"

When he got closer to the fire, he saw that all the monkeys were dancing on the burning trees and bushes in an attempt to smother the flames. Oakee also jumped with them. Great whirlwinds of smoke gusted about the edges of the firestorm. The smoke kept getting in his face so that he often had to hold his breath and close his eyes. It was in exactly one of these moments, when his eyes were shut tight to keep out the smoke, that he felt a terrific *whack* on the side of his head, and everything went black.

When Oakee woke up, the first thing he saw was Lulu the colorful hummingbird sitting on the end of Airavata's long, white trunk; and the first thing he heard was . . . jingle-bells! He tried to sit up, but a pain shot through his head, so he lay back down. He touched the side of his head and found it covered with a bunch of wet leaves.

"Good morning sleepy-head!" peeped Lulu merrily. "You had a nice time last night; that is, until that tree knocked you over. Hanuman was very proud of you. You helped put out that wicked ego-fire! He brought us here to this river, and then he flew to get the sanjivakarani leaves for your wound. They're soaked in the holy water of this river. It's called Ganga. Do you feel better?"

Lulu was talking so fast that it only served to make Oakee's headache worse. But as soon as she stopped, the soft gurgling of the water and the jingling of the tiny bells soothed him again.

When he started to feel better, he answered, "I'm

alright, Lu. But where are Hanuman and his helpers? I did so want to play with them some more."

"He said he would like to accompany us, but that there are many more emergencies which he must attend to," explained Lulu. "He said we will stay cool and safe if we follow this river. Are you ready to go?"

"I'm as ready as I'll ever be," replied Oakee. "Let's hurry before something else happens!"

CHAPTER 13

Gobbledy's Ego

The place on the sacred river where Oakee woke up was actually the northern edge of the Jingle Jungle. Here the blossoming trees and bushes were still lush and beautiful, kept alive by the pure vibrations of the river water. However, their journey was now to lead them away from the graces of nature, and into the hostile and unnatural world of modern civilization. Despite the motherly love of this great river, selfish people treated her with disrespect and greed. Oakee and his friends were appalled by the ugliness which met them on their way along her banks.

The first shock occurred as they left the sweetness of the forest and found themselves approaching a small industrial town. In the distance, they could see black smoke filling the hot sky, and as they got closer, Oakee noticed that the river water was looking oily. As he stared down at the grimy water, a big, dirty crocodile suddenly jumped out of it right onto their path! Airavata stopped so abruptly that Oakee lost his balance and went tumbling down to the ground. When he lifted his head, he was looking right into the face of the crocodile. Normally, Oakee would have been so scared that he would have started crying; but instead, he started laughing. The reason was that this old crocodile was wearing a man's hat on his head, which made him look so ridiculous that Oakee couldn't help laughing out loud. In a moment Lulu and Airavata were also chuckling.

"How dare you laugh in my presence!" growled the vain old reptile. "I am the great Gobbledy, river-chief of Gandapur. Aren't you afraid of me?!"

"Well, I would be," giggled Oakee, "if you didn't look so silly!" When he said this, Lulu and Airavata laughed even louder.

When the crocodile noticed that they were laughing at his hat, he announced indignantly, "It may worry you to know that this was the hat of a big factory boss who I ate for lunch one day. No one may pass this way without paying toll to Gobbledy. What will you offer me?"

Lulu couldn't resist teasing the selfish old beast, so she flew onto his nose and giggled, "We would certainly make a generous payment for your blessings, oh, great Gobbledy, but you seem to have everything anyone could ever wish for."

At this, the three of them burst into a frenzy of laughter. Then, in a fit of rage, the old crocodile did something that no one was ready for. In the wink of an eye he had opened his big mouth and snapped it shut, with Lulu inside! Oakee jumped to his feet and screamed, but the wise and ancient Airavata sprung instantly into the air and came down on the crocodile's tail. The big mouth opened and out shot Lulu like a bullet. Gobbledy the crocodile slithered into the oily water and was never seen or heard by anyone again.

Lulu rested in Oakee's hand, her little heart still beating wildly.

"Are you okay, Lu?!" asked Oakee with an anxious voice. When she had caught her breath and stopped shaking, he added, "That will teach you not to tickle the ego of an old dinosaur."

"Even the dinosaurs are developing egos then?" Lulu chirped. "Did you see his face when he defended that old hat? I think he must have been possessed by that factory boss's ghost!"

Remembering the indignant look on the crocodile's face, they all burst out laughing again. And hearing Airavata's laugh made Oakee and Lulu laugh even harder.

(If you ever heard an elephant laugh, you would know why.) When they had calmed down and Oakee and Lulu were back up in their places, the three travelers set out again along the river.

Nighttime was drawing near as they passed under the shadows of the factories. The few people they saw from a distance seemed too busy to take notice of them. And so they passed silently through their first night among the blind masses of men.

CHAPTER 14

The Forgiveness Mantra

Oakee woke up early the next morning, scratching himself.

"Ugh! It seems we've found the mosquitoes – or they've found us," he mumbled.

Lulu yawned and stretched on Oakee's lap. Airavata was still walking steadily along. They had crossed through two more human settlements in the night, and now they were approaching the first city on their journey. As far as the eye could see, the hard shapes of manmade buildings peered out from the early morning river mists before them. Soon the unearthly noises of automobiles met the three travelers. They began seeing more and more people rushing around. It was all like a joyless dance with noise instead of music, thought Oakee. The people saw the travelers as a dirty boy on a dirty old elephant, not as a prince on the divine vehicle of the king of the heavens. The city dogs barked angrily at them as they passed, but Airavata simply waved his big white ears, which sent a cooling wind over them.

On and on they went until at last, choked by the heavy air, Oakee said, "I'm so thirsty and hungry. Where can we find something to eat and drink?"

They were just passing a busy fruit market, so Airavata did the most spontaneous and natural thing – he reached over to one of the stands, picked up the biggest, juiciest piece of fruit, and passed it up to Prince Oakee. Oakee and Lulu gobbled it down. But before they could finish their nice breakfast, they heard shouting from down below. Oakee looked down and saw a crowd of angry faces calling up at him. One man with a black turban and a big black beard was shaking his fist. Oakee couldn't understand what he was saying, or what the whole fuss was about.

Suddenly, the man started kicking Airavata's leg. Airavata didn't mind, but it was too much for Oakee. He jumped down from the elephant's back and landed right on the man's foot. This was too much for the angry man, who quickly grabbed Oakee by the ear and began dragging him away through the crowd, shouting something about stealing his fruit, and going to the police. This, in turn, was too much for Lulu, who flew into the man's face and started pecking his nose. Someone grabbed her and pushed her into a cloth sack. Airavata gave a mighty trumpet blast and tried to follow Oakee, but the people picked up stones and threw them at the elephant.

The situation was getting completely out of control and would have ended in disaster, if not for a certain miracle. King Varuna had given Oakee a boon, a special weapon that would save him from aggressive people. It was a very powerful mantra, a chant, which he had told Lulu to give to Oakee. Unfortunately, she had forgotten to tell him about it.

So, it is not difficult to understand why, when Oakee shouted, "Lu! Lu! What should we do!" and Lulu shouted back from inside the sack, "Use the Aparadhakshama Astra – the weapon of forgiveness!" that Oakee hadn't the faintest idea what she was talking about.

But luckily, just before Oakee was dragged out of earshot, Lulu quickly added, "You know! Say you forgive everyone!"

Oakee felt cool vibrations on his hands and head when he heard this, so he didn't waste a moment. He immediately took a deep breath and called out loud from his heart: "I FORGIVE EVERYONE!" And that's when the miracle happened!

Everyone there on the scene suddenly became silent, as if a big pillow had dropped down from heaven and buried all the noise. Not even the roaring of the rush-hour traffic could be heard. The dark, hairy man let go of Oakee's ear and started kissing the little boy's hands, as big tears rolled out of his eyes. The person who held Lulu prisoner quickly opened the sack to let her fly out. People were pulling their own ears as a gesture of apology, or gently stroking the elephant, or offering food and drink to Oakee and his companions. Loaded with a feast of goodies, Oakee was then helped back up onto Airavata; and everyone smiled and waved and said 'good-bye' (which really means 'God-be-with-you') as the three set off along the riverbank towards the top of the world.

After a little while of eating and meditating, Oakee said, "Hey, Lu. Why didn't you tell me about that astra?"

"I just did," she answered smartly.

"Okay. I forgive *you* too, you naughty little bird."

CHAPTER 15

Blessings From the Mother Empress

Although Airavata walked slowly, they seemed to cover great distances quickly. This is a special power, or 'siddhi,' of the divine vahana-vehicles of the deva-gods; they can carry their masters very far in a short time. It was only when they passed through densely populated areas that their progress diminished significantly (that is: when a lot of people were around, they seemed to move more slowly). And unfortunately, due to the tremendous ego-heat in the people, Oakee and his friends were often scorned and harassed as they journeyed through these areas of dense population.

One evening, as they were leaving one such disheartening place, the circumstances took an even harder turn for the worse as five mean robbers blocked the travelers' path on the riverbank. It was not entirely clear what they wanted, but they ordered Oakee to get down off the elephant. Oakee was not frightened, but he was so tired and frustrated by all the aggression they had already encountered, that he just sunk his head and prayed to his Heavenly Mother Empress to save him from this torture.

Then another miracle happened! Out of nowhere a huge tiger came lunging at the robbers. His magnificent coat shone fiery red in the light of the setting sun, and his roar shook the evening air like thunder. The five men turned and ran for their lives, and were soon out of sight. The tiger also disappeared, but it went ahead of Airavata for the rest of their journey, and no one tried to trouble them again. Oakee sometimes caught glimpses of the big, striped cat going before them by the dim light of morning or late evening; and whenever he saw it he would smile and secretly thank the loving Empress of the Universe in his heart.

The second half of their land journey was less eventful. Airavata traveled always near to the heavenly river to protect Oakee and Lulu from getting burned by the increasing heat of the collective ego that grew with the anger and greed in men's heads. They rarely stopped, and they saw less and less people as they neared the mountains. Oakee often wondered what awaited him at the journey's end on top of the world. Lulu told him many amazing stories about what she had seen in the realm of the devas, and Oakee dreamed colorful dreams of things that he didn't understand.

One morning he woke up and looked around from the back of Airavata. The river had been growing smaller as they ascended into the mountains. Now it was a shining, bubbling brook that laughed happily between its grassy banks. It seemed to him that they were going back in time and seeing the heavenly Ganga as a young maiden, dancing in the dawn of the world.

Everything was so magical up here! One beautiful feeling after another rose up from deep within Oakee as he watched the first pink sunlight touch the snowy mountain peaks; or he breathed in the delicate perfumes of the countless flowers that smiled on the slopes; or listened to the laughter of the river that seemed to be calling him to dance. He felt young and old, tiny and big, all at the same time. The heavens of the devas had been a lovely place, he thought, but this earthly home of the divine Mother Empress must be more beautiful than all the other heavens put together. As his mind danced lightly from sweet thought to sweet thought, a happy humming sound suddenly caught his attention. It was Lulu. He hadn't even noticed that she was away. She had been out collecting breakfast.

"I've brought you some nectar from the Valley of Flowers," she sang. We're climbing the Nanda Devi, the mountain of the Heavenly Mother. Isn't it all so exciting?!"

Oakee could only giggle in response. Lulu's bubbling enthusiasm tickled his heart. He was so glad that she had been with him from the beginning of his adventures. Would he ever see her again when their mission was fulfilled, he wondered?

Up and up and up they climbed. Every moment was a drop of pure joy in Oakee's heart. Time seemed to be standing still as they reached the snowy regions, high above the tree line. On and on Airavata trudged through the white wonderland. The rest of the planet Earth seemed to grow smaller and smaller below them. Oakee had peacefully stopped breathing. His whole being was spread open like a lotus in full bloom. A few more steps and they would be above the sky; above the universe; above the whole of Creation. And then . . .

CHAPTER 16

Meditation With the Mother

As they reached the utmost peak of Nanda Devi, the thousand petal lotus of the universe – the Sahasrara, the Crown of Creation – stretched out before them, one golden peak more beautiful than the next. The silence and splendor of that moment was suddenly accompanied by a little sound. At first Oakee couldn't comprehend what it was; then he realized that Lulu was talking to him again.

"That must be the great Mount Kailash way over there," she was saying, "and that blue spot must be the magic lake. But if Ganga came to the Earth over there, how did she get way over here?"

She was still talking as something wondrous began to happen. From far over the many valleys and peaks that separated them from their ultimate destination, they could faintly make out a colorful line growing in the morning sunlight. The line grew nearer and nearer to them until it occurred to them what it was.

"The rainbow!" exclaimed Lulu.

As the rainbow came closer, they could see something white on the end of it. Lulu was just starting to shout, "It's the cow!" when Oakee grabbed her beak, as he felt it would be disrespectful to shout in the presence of this divine being.

When the Cow and the Rainbow reached the place where they stood, Oakee bowed and the Cow smiled at him, saying:

"Blessed child of our Heavenly Mother, welcome to the kingdom of Nirananda. I have the great privilege to guide you into the sacred Heart of this home of the Mother. Please follow me."

As Airavata stepped onto the rainbow with his passengers, Lulu whispered, "I bet Ganga came over to here on the rainbow." And, with that important remark, she remained quiet for the rest of the adventure.

The lush valleys and majestic peaks passed beneath them as they went. The rainbow was leading them gracefully downward in the direction of the Queen of All Lakes; the first Water to refresh the Earth at the beginning of time, at the foot of Lord Shiva's white throne, Mount Kailash. Oakee soon saw miles and miles of warm, bare earth, which rolled away from the brilliant sapphire Sea and the timeless Mountain. They were almost there. A delicious coolness bathed his skin and flowed through his veins. Airavata's feet met the ground with the lightness of a feather. Everything was still and in a state of absolute silence. The Cow and the Rainbow had vanished.

Airavata helped Oakee down. They were on the shore of the divine lake now. She looked like a bottomless sky spread out on the Earth. Oakee sat down on the bare ground beside her. For a time, whether it was long or short he could not tell, he just sat there staring at her. Then he closed his eyes, or someone closed them for him. The next thing he noticed was a soft, motherly voice. It seemed to come from within him. It was singing . . . something like a lullaby. He began to understand the words.

They said he should *find the Divine Pearl in the heights of his being . . . he should ride the Heavenly River inside himself . . . let go of everything hard and heavy* (even the idea that anything could be 'hard' or 'heavy' seemed impossible to him in this moment) . . . *he should take the hand of his Heavenly Mother . . . with his other hand he should grasp the hand of humanity . . . open the shell . . . share the Pearl. . . .*

The song continued, and Oakee followed each sweet drop of it like a baby taking milk from its mother. He was going deeper and deeper within his heart; and at the same time, rising higher and higher. He felt all the glory of his own true Being revealed to him. Still deeper and higher his attention went. He wanted never to be separated from this feeling of perfect delight. He felt he must be very near the treasure now. He wanted to share it with everyone!

Then he saw it: A flawless pearl-heart of pure joy! He touched it and it became countless doves that flew out over the world. He saw silent, cascading fireworks lighting the skies with a thousand colors, and fountains of molten gold that decorated the heavens with joyful majesty. The Cool Breeze of Heavenly Love bathed the three worlds, and the Creation smiled like a baby sleeping in its Mother's arms.

CHAPTER 17

The Saving Grace

Oakee felt so wonderful in that sweet, silent joy, that he didn't want to open his eyes ever again; but when he did, he found that he was all wet. And, to add to his surprise, it became clear that the Lake was rising and taking him with her! The divine water was ascending in such a way that it didn't flood the whole valley, but rose in a column toward the sky. The top of the water became wider and wider like a mushroom cloud. Oakee was being lifted right up into the clouds. He was still so puffed up with the joyful vibrations from his meditation, that he felt a little bit like a cloud himself. The water mingled with all the clouds and spread out further and further. This went on and on till Oakee thought it must have been covering the whole world.

Then Oakee saw a flash of lightning and heard a growl of thunder that sounded like a giant tiger. He looked up and saw King Indra on Airavata between Avartaka and Pushkala. His favorite rain clouds were now dark and brimming with cool, vibrating water. Oakee waved and the King of Devalok smiled and waved in reply.

A moment later, Oakee was to be the first human being ever to have a hands-on experience of a cloudburst – the clouds literally *burst* beneath him, and down, down, down he went with the divine rain towards the angry, thirsty world below. Knowing that all the people would feel new lightness and coolness in their heads, and healing love in their hearts, he closed his eyes and began singing one of the lovely tunes he had learned with the gandharva angels in the sun clouds, what seemed such a long time ago.

When he opened his eyes again, Oakee found himself on the swing in his garden. It was still Sunday, and the kitchen bell was ringing to call him in for lunch. It was starting to rain, so he jumped off the swing and ran to the house. Before he ran, he had looked up at the rain and thought he had seen a colorful little hummingbird eating from a blossom on the apple tree above the swings.

When he reached the house he went straight to the bathroom to wash his hands. On the way, he wondered if his whole adventure had just been a daydream; but when he looked into the mirror, he saw the scratch on the side of his head where the burning tree had hit him as he danced with

Hanuman and his monkey-angels in the Jingle Jungle.

~GLOSSARY~

Astra
A divine weapon, used to defeat evil.

Auspicious
Happening in the best possible way, at the best possible time.

Bandhan
A powerful, divine hand gesture (writing an invisible message on the open left hand with a finger, then making many clockwise circles over it with the open right hand) that telephones the angels to help. It can also be used as a protection, by passing the right hand seven times over the body, back and forth from side to side over the head.

Deva
A (normally invisible) god that takes care of the elements.

Devi
Goddess.

Devalok or Amaravati
Celestial kingdom of the devas.

Ego

The balloon in a person's head that gets very big and hot, hurting others, if one gets too selfish or angry. (It shrinks down to its normal size if we are generous and kind. Doing this creates cool, healing *Vibrations* in us and others.)

Ganga
The primordial, divine river that flows through northern India (also, the goddess who created this river).

Garuda
The divine vahana (vehicle) of Lord Vishnu, destroyer of evil and poisons, and king of the birds.

Heavenly Mother Empress
Highest benevolent ruler of all worlds and beings. (Mother is the highest person there can be; Empress is the highest ruler there can be; and Heavenly is the highest quality there can be.) She brings joy and peace to anyone who remembers Her in their heart.

Indra
King of the devas and the lower heavens, and master of the weather.

Indrani
Consort and shakti (female power) of King Indra.

Jai
Victory!

Kailash
Mountain in the Himalayas known as the seat of Lord Shiva.

Lord Shiva
Fatherly deity, protector of the precious heart-spirit of the universe, and in all people.

Lord Ganesha
Elephant-headed child deity made of earth and divine vibrations, protector of the Earth and innocence in everyone.

Lord Hanuman (or Hanumana)
Leader of the (normally invisible) angels, and messenger of the gods.

Lord Vishnu
Protecting deity and guide of evolution.

Mantra
A divine hymn or chant that brings powerful blessings when sung or spoken.

Meditation

Being very peaceful, happy and full of energy, with no noisey thoughts in the head (different than being normally awake or asleep).

Nirananda

Silent, absolute joy.

Om

Powerful primordial sound of the Creation.

Rakshasa

An evil, trouble-making demon.

Sahasrara

The beautiful rainbow lotus at the top of Creation and on top of every person's head – the ultimate door to Heaven.

Vahana

Divine vehicle.

Varuna

King of the water realms.

Vibrations (or Chaitanya)

The divine power that created everything. It can be felt on the hands and the top of the head of an enlightened person as a cool breeze.

Oakee's mother told him long, long ago (last summer) that if he ever wanted to help *happy* the world, he should start with himself. Then she showed him how to look into his heart to get strong and free. Whenever he closes his eyes and opens his hands, with the palms flat facing heaven, he can feel a soft cool breeze coming out of them and the top of his head. Then he feels his heart shine with peace and happiness. When you're following him on his adventures, you can see if you too can feel these special powers. And then you can see if others can also feel this flow of heavenly love. As a prince or princess of the Heavenly Mother Empress, it is your right to enjoy this – to really enjoy your Self and others.

By the way, if you follow the . . .

. . . mouse footprints, they just might . . .

. . . lead you to the next . . .

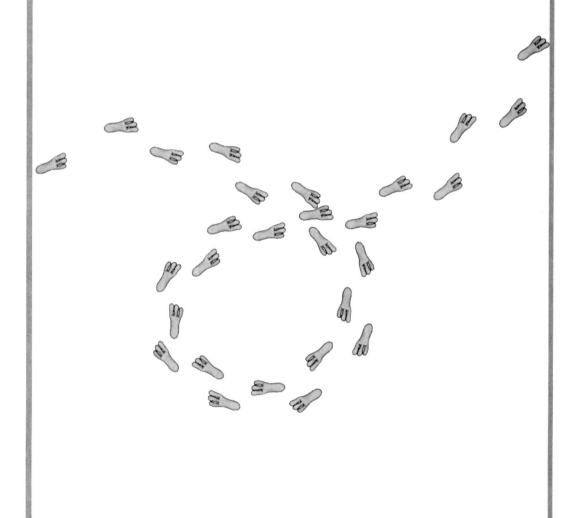

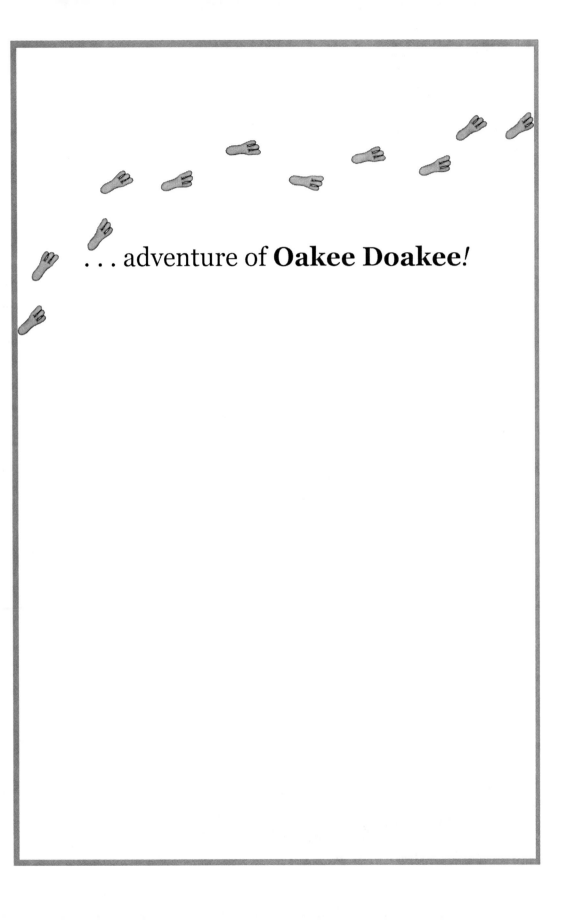

. . . adventure of **Oakee Doakee***!*

Printed in the United States
118023LV00003B/51-100/P

9 780955 150364